WARE

Ghostville Elementary®

Frighting Like Cats and Dogs

Find out more spooky secrets about

Ghostville Elementary®

Ghostville Elementary®

Frighting Like Cats and Dogs

by Marcia Thornton Jones
and
Debbie Dadey

illustrated by Guy Francis

A
LITTLE APPLE
PAPERBACK

SCHOLASTIC INC.
New York   Toronto   London   Auckland   Sydney
Mexico City   New Delhi   Hong Kong   Buenos Aires

*To Alecia Marcum, Mitchie Neel, Cindy Williams, Beth Luttrell,
Kathy Cook, and to all librarians, reading teachers, and curriculum
specialists everywhere who know how to make reading fun—
and how to make authors welcome in their schools!*

—MTJ

*To Gerrie and her dream. And to Vickie Hall and Linda Fredericks
who work so hard to keep Gerrie's dream alive in Ottawa, Kansas.
Also, to Alecia Marcum, librarian extraordinaire in Bowling Green,
Kentucky, and to Mitchie Neel who makes reading so special in
Blount County, Alabama.*

—DD

ISBN 0-439-88359-8

12 11 10 9 8 7 6 5 4 3 2 1   6 7 8 9 10 11/0

Printed in the U.S.A.   40
First printing, October 2006

Contents

THE LEGEND

Sleepy Hollow Elementary School's
Online Newspaper

This Just In: Dogs and Cats
Run Crazy in Haunted Basement

Breaking News: A monster dog almost ate a defenseless white cat this week when the third graders washed pets to raise money for the animal shelter. Mr. Morton tried to save the cat by wearing it on his head, but the dog chased the cat all the way to the haunted woods. This reporter bets a ghost spooked the dog out of the basement. I'd run, too, if someone tried to give me a bath in that creepy classroom. But the day wasn't a total loss, because Mr. Morton's class raised lots of cash for the local animal shelter. Who says kids can't make a difference? Stay tuned for more breaking news as it develops.

Your friendly fifth-grade reporter,
Justin Thyme

1
Gato

"We have to find him," Nina told Jeff and Cassidy. The three friends were walking down the sidewalk on their way to the animal shelter.

"We will," Jeff said. "How many fat orange cats can there be in Sleepy Hollow?"

"My *abuela* cried herself to sleep last night," Nina admitted to her buddies. "Her cat has never run away before, and it's all my fault!"

"No, it's not," Cassidy shook her blond head. "You can't help it if your grandmother's cat ran out when you opened the door."

"Don't worry," Jeff said. "If Gato isn't at the animal shelter, we'll get every third grader at school to help us look."

Nina smiled. "You're the best friends anyone could ever have."

Jeff shrugged. "I know."

"Okay," Cassidy said as they walked up to the short brick building. "Let's find your grandmother's cat." Cassidy held the door open for her friends.

"Phew-ew!" Jeff said. "This place stinks."

"Jeff!" Cassidy said. "That's rude."

Jeff shook his head. "No, it's the truth."

It was the truth. Not only did the animal shelter smell worse than a pig farm, it looked like a hurricane had just gone through. Cages were stacked everywhere. Each cage was filled with a cat, dog, rabbit, or duck. There were large cages, small cages, and a few dogs were even tied to a small desk. A big gray dog barked at the kids. Soon all the dogs were howling or barking. Nina stood behind Cassidy, away from the noisy dogs.

A very small old lady sat at the desk talking on the phone. She had to yell

2

to be heard over the noise. "No," she said into the phone. "We haven't had any new cats brought in for a week. And if we did, I don't know where we'd put them."

Nina felt like crying. She had so hoped to find her grandmother's missing cat.

"Come on," Jeff said, tugging on Nina's arm. "We might as well leave."

Cassidy held up her hand. "We're not going anywhere."

"Didn't you hear?" Jeff asked. "They don't have any new cats."

"This place is a mess," Cassidy said. "We need to help that lady."

"What about Gato?" Nina said.

"We'll help for a little while, and then we'll hunt for Gato," Cassidy explained.

As soon as the lady put down the phone, Cassidy introduced herself. "Hi, I'm Cassidy. These are my friends, Nina and Jeff. We're here to help."

"Oh my, aren't you lifesavers? I'm

Mrs. Hudson. There are cleaning sup-
plies in that closet."

Nina helped Mrs. Hudson clean the
cages. Cassidy scooped out litterboxes.
Jeff gave all the animals fresh water, but
he stopped working when he came to an
Irish Setter. The card on the cage door
said the dog's name was Red.

Red poked his nose through the cage
and licked Jeff's hand. He looked up at
Jeff with big brown eyes. Jeff had always
wanted a dog. A dog just like Red.

2
No Dogs!

After visiting the animal shelter, Nina and her friends searched for Gato all afternoon. They looked in backyards. They knocked on doors. They even looked in gutters. No Gato. Everywhere they went they put up signs. By the time Nina got home, her grandmother was so upset she wouldn't eat dinner. Nina just had to find that cat!

The next day at school, Nina was so sad she couldn't keep her mind on her school work. Jeff didn't feel much better. He frowned during math class. He stared out the window when Mr. Morton read them a story. He put his head on his desk during spelling.

"Pssst," Nina whispered. "Are you sick?"

Jeff shrugged. He did feel sick. He wanted Red so badly that his stomach ached. The problem was that his mom always said, "No stinky dogs!" There had to be a way to get his mother to let him adopt Red.

Cassidy felt sorry for both of her friends, but she couldn't forget all the homeless animals. She kept thinking about their sad eyes.

During social studies, Jeff was day-dreaming about playing fetch with Red

when Mr. Morton pointed to a map of Sleepy Hollow. "Here we are on our state map. This month we'll be thinking about what it means to be a good citizen."

Cassidy raised her hand. "Mr. Morton, isn't it important for us to help in our community?"

Mr. Morton wiped chalk dust away from his glasses and nodded. "That's part

of being a good citizen. Can anyone think of ways to help?"

Carla's and Darla's hands shot up into the air. The twins were always ready with an answer.

Before Mr. Morton could call on anyone a boy named Andrew blurted out, "We could storm city hall and demand a skateboard park."

Mr. Morton frowned, but Carla waved her hand and said, "We could plant flowers . . ."

Her twin sister Darla finished the sentence, ". . . when it gets warmer."

"That's an excellent idea," Mr. Morton agreed.

"I know something we could do right now," Cassidy said, "but it might be a little hard."

Andrew groaned. He hated to do anything that made him work.

"We could raise money for the animal shelter," Cassidy said. "Jeff, Nina, and I were there yesterday and it was a mess."

"We were looking for my grandmother's cat," Nina explained. "He ran away two days ago. Has anyone seen a big orange cat?"

Everyone in the classroom shook their heads.

Jeff, seeing how sad Nina looked, said, "We need everybody to help us look for him after school."

"I'll certainly keep an eye out for that cat," Mr. Morton told Nina. "Now, how could we raise money for the shelter?"

"We could have a bake sale," Darla suggested.

"We could make signs for donations," Cassidy said. She loved using her computer to make things.

Jeff raised his hand. He remembered how stinky all the animals were at the shelter. "Instead of a car wash, we could have a pet wash."

Mr. Morton made a list on the board. "These are all great ideas. I think we should do them all!"

The class clapped and cheered, except for Andrew. He slid down in his chair. The idea of stinky wet dogs did not make him happy.

Someone else wasn't happy, either. Someone who floated above the classroom listening to the kids' ideas. That someone was a ghost.

3
Pet Bath Day

"We can have the pet wash right here in our classroom," said Carla.

"On a Saturday," added Darla.

"Do we have to?" Andrew groaned.

Mr. Morton shook his head. "Of course not, but I'll give extra credit to anyone that helps."

Andrew slid down in his seat until his chin rested on the desk. He needed all the extra credit he could get.

"We can make signs and invite everyone in the neighborhood," Nina said.

"We'll call it Sleepy Hollow's Pet Bath Day," Cassidy added. She sat down at a computer and typed out all of the ideas. Well, *almost* all of the ideas. She didn't add the comments she heard from the ceiling.

Everyone in Sleepy Hollow told stories about the school basement being haunted, but to most they were just make-believe. Only Cassidy, Nina, and Jeff knew the truth. The ghosts were real, but for some reason they only let the three friends see or hear them.

"Nooooooooooo," screeched a ghost girl named Calliope huddled in the back of the room. She had a long braid tied with a bow and cuddled a black ghost cat in her arms. "Cocomo is afraid of other animals," Calliope said.

A ghost boy with overalls and a missing tooth floated nearby. It was Ozzy. His hands were balled into fists and his head had grown to the size of a watermelon. A shaggy dog hunkered beneath Ozzy, his tail firmly tucked between his legs. The ghost dog looked up at Ozzy with worried eyes. "Huxley is the only dog allowed in this room!" the ghost boy bellowed, causing the papers on Mr. Morton's desk to flutter to the floor.

"Shhh," Jeff hissed.

"Don't tell me to be quiet," Andrew told him.

"I wasn't talking to you," Jeff said.

"Then who were you talking to?" Andrew asked.

Jeff wanted to tell the whole school about the ghosts, but he knew that if he did they would think he had lost his marbles. Instead of telling the class about the ghosts, he shook his head. "Nobody," he said. It wasn't a total lie, since as far as ghosts were concerned there was "no body."

For the rest of the week, the ghosts muttered and mumbled as the third graders made their plans. Cassidy used a classroom computer to print signs. They told about Pet Bath Day, and also asked for help finding Gato. The posters were hung up around town. Kids organized door-to-door advertising campaigns. The fifth grade even wrote about the third grade's fund-raising project in the school newspaper.

Meanwhile, Nina asked everyone they talked to if they had seen her grandmother's missing cat. Nobody had. Every place they searched turned up cat-less, too.

Bright and early on Saturday morning, customers lined up outside the playground door that led to the basement classroom of Sleepy Hollow Elementary. There were dogs that needed baths, cats that needed brushing, and even some hamster cages that needed fresh cedar chips. There was even a bright blue fish. "I just hate cleaning out Moby's bowl," the fish owner explained. "I'll pick him up after I go to the grocery store."

Andrew grabbed the hamster's cage. "I'll take the rat," he said.

The hamster's person gasped. "My Chuckles is no rat," he said.

"Whatever," Andrew muttered.

Carla and Darla helped each other carry Moby's bowl.

Jeff volunteered to help bathe dogs. So far, he hadn't seen a single dog like Red.

Cassidy entered each person's name in a computer as they entered the classroom, along with the pet's name and what the pet needed. As people dropped off their pets, Nina asked them if they had seen her grandmother's cat. No one had found a big orange cat.

Mr. Morton hurried from group to group, making sure everything went smoothly and that no pet was upset.

The room quickly filled up with animals and kids. That wasn't all. There were also ghosts. Calliope huddled on top of a bookcase, cuddling her black ghost cat, Cocomo. Becky and Ozzy zoomed from corner to corner.

Huxley, Ozzy's ghost dog, took one look at a Great Dane that Jeff was brushing and started howling. "*A-wooooooooo! A-wooooooooo!*"

What was worse, the Great Dane seemed to be able to see the ghost dog. And Huxley wasn't the only ghost the Great Dane saw. He also saw Cocomo, the ghost cat.

The giant dog took one look at the black ghost cat and lunged. Jeff tried to hold on, but the leash slipped from his hand.

"Get that dog!" Cassidy yelled.

The Great Dane jumped over the fuzzy white cat being brushed by Nina

and knocked over the hamster cage. Chuckles's cage burst open. Out skittered the hamster.

"*Grrrrrrrrrrr,*" growled the Great Dane as it jumped for Cocomo's ghost tail.

"*Phhhhhht,*" hissed Cocomo.

"*A-wooooooooooo!*" howled Huxley.

"*Reorrrrrrr,*" yowled the fuzzy white cat.

"Catch those animals," Mr. Morton yelled. He didn't know that Ozzy was

waving his fingers in front of the white cat. His fingers squirmed like ten long snakes. The cat swatted its paw at Ozzy.

The white cat hunkered down. She wiggled her tail. Then she pounced ... right on top of Mr. Morton's head.

4
Snake Fingers

"AAAAAAAARRRRRRRRRRRRGH!" screamed Mr. Morton. He turned. He twirled. He hopped. No matter what he did, the white cat hung on to his head.

Ozzy waved his snake-fingers in front of the white cat again. Cocomo leaped off the bookshelves at Ozzy's wiggling fingers.

The Great Dane chased the ghostly shadow cat.

Huxley, of course, ran after the Great Dane.

"Look out!" Cassidy screamed as the two dogs and Cocomo landed right at their teacher's feet.

"AAAAAAAAAAAAAAAHHHHHH!" screamed Mr. Morton.

"AAAAAAAAAAAAAAHHHHHH!" screamed the kids in the class.

"A-WOOOOOOOOOOOOOOOO!" howled Huxley as Mr. Morton toppled to the ground.

Their teacher lay on the floor, tangled in tails, whiskers, and paws. Just then, the door crashed open. Or maybe it banged. There stood Olivia.

Ozzy, Huxley, and Cocomo jumped through the wall and disappeared after one look at Olivia. Olivia had been the head custodian of Sleepy Hollow Elementary since before anybody could remember. The kids were used to seeing her red overalls and tool belt. They were also used to Olivia carrying around animals.

Andrew pointed to the creature in her arms. "Is that a rat wearing armor?" he asked.

"Amos is no more a rat than you are," Olivia said as she stroked the hard head of the animal in her arms.

"Looks like a rat to me," Andrew muttered.

"Amos is an armadillo, and he's not wearing armor," Olivia said as she surveyed the mess in the room. "This is bone. It helps protect Amos, but unfortunately it means poor Amos isn't very flexible. He can't bend or adapt the way the rest of us can."

Then Olivia looked down at Mr. Morton. The white cat still sat on his head. Its tail swished slowly back and forth across the teacher's glasses.

"That is a most unusual hat you're wearing," Olivia said.

"We're trying to raise money to help homeless animals," Cassidy explained while Nina gently lifted the cat off Mr. Morton's head. Carla and Darla helped their teacher up while Andrew grabbed the Great Dane's collar.

"We're also hoping someone will have seen my grandmother's orange cat," Nina added.

"It's not going very well," Jeff said. "The animals seem a bit upset."

Olivia tilted her head to one side and her earrings jingled. Or maybe they jangled. "Some animals, like Amos here, find it hard to share their space."

"But these animals don't belong here," Andrew sputtered.

"They have to get along, or the entire project will be a flop," Cassidy added.

"Each animal has feelings, just like people do," Olivia said. "Maybe if you  keep that in mind, everything will work much better." With that, Olivia and Amos disappeared into the dark shadows of Ghostville Elementary's basement.

5
Streak of Orange

Nina brushed the white cat and it purred in her lap. "I wish you were my grandmother's cat," Nina whispered. The ghost cat, Cocomo, rubbed up against Nina's leg. Nina tried to scratch the ghost cat's neck, but her hand passed right through Cocomo's ear instead. Nina shivered at the sudden cold of a ghost against her fingers.

Cocomo plopped a brown string in Nina's lap and the white cat batted at it with her paw. "So, you want to be friends?" Nina asked Cocomo. "That's a good girl." The white cat grabbed the string in her mouth and Cocomo batted at it. Soon they were playing like old buddies.

Together, Cassidy and Jeff held the

huge Great Dane in a baby bathtub. Cassidy kept the giant dog distracted by letting it sniff an old piece of wood. Huxley watched every move she made because the piece of wood was his toy. He'd been chasing it for over a hundred years, but he seemed happy to share for the moment.

Carla and Darla rubbed the Great Dane with soapy water.

"You're a good doggy," Jeff told the dog. "Just like Red." What Carla and

Darla didn't know was that Jeff was also talking to the ghost dog. Huxley licked Jeff's hand, sending a rash of goose bumps flying up his arm.

Olivia had been right. The ghost animals were fine as long as the kids remembered to pay attention to them, too.

"Thank goodness we finally got all these animals to calm down," Cassidy said, looking around the room. There had to be at least ten dogs and cats being

brushed or washed by the third-grade kids in the classroom. Andrew had even managed to get the hamster back in its cage. Mr. Morton sat at his desk rubbing his head.

"The worst is over," Carla said.

Darla nodded and poured a cup of clean water over the Great Dane's back. "All we have to do now is collect the money for the shelter. This was a good idea."

Jeff smiled and relaxed his grip on the big dog. He just hoped this pet wash would somehow help Nina find Gato. Maybe one of the pet owners would be able to help them.

Jeff didn't notice that the very cat they'd been looking for was sunning itself on the school windowsill. None of the other kids noticed, either. The Great Dane, however, spotted the fat orange cat. When Andrew opened the outside door to let in another pet owner, the big dog leaped.

Nina and the white cat sat in the way.

"Ahhh!" Nina screamed as the dog knocked her down. The white cat screeched and raced out the door ahead of the Great Dane. Huxley and Cocomo couldn't resist the fun and they ran out the door, too.

"Shut the door before all the pets get away!" Jeff yelled as dogs barked all over the room.

"Oh, no!" Mr. Morton said. "We have to catch those pets before their owners get back."

"I'll get them," Nina said in a rush. "I think I saw a streak of orange. I bet that big dog is chasing Gato."

"Jeff and I will go, too," Cassidy offered.

"Don't go past the playground," Mr. Morton warned. "I hope you can find them. Their owners will be back soon and they'll be very upset." He took off his glasses and rubbed them with a tissue.

Carla put her hands on her hips. "This was the worst idea . . ."

"Ever," Darla agreed.

6
Dog Lunch

A spine-chilling wail echoed throughout the classroom. Green glitter sparkled in front of Nina. The glitter swirled until it took the form of the ghost named Calliope. Her long braid floated above her head. "Find my cat," she moaned.

"Don't worry, we'll find Cocomo," Nina told the ghost.

"Who is Cocomo?" Mr. Morton asked as he looked over the list of pet names Cassidy had entered into the computer.

Nina turned red and realized that everyone had heard her talking to the ghost. She knew there was no pet named Cocomo on the list. "I've been calling the white cat Cocomo," Nina fibbed, crossing her fingers behind her back.

"OOOOHHHHHHH! I must have my Cocomo," wailed Calliope. She reached long thin arms out to Nina. A numbing coldness filled Nina and she shuddered.

Calliope put her hands to her face and sobbed. The tears formed a huge puddle around her feet. Calliope's moans continued as she melted into the tears. In just a few seconds, Calliope was a puddle on the floor. Her wails and moans still filled the classroom, but only Jeff, Cassidy, and Nina could hear them.

"You'd better hurry," Mr. Morton said. "Slip out the door quickly before we lose any more pets."

"I'll go, too," Andrew said.

Mr. Morton shook his head. "No." He knew that if there was trouble to be found, Andrew would certainly find it. More trouble was the last thing they needed. "Hurry," Mr. Morton told Jeff, Cassidy, and Nina as they squeezed out the door that led to the playground.

The kids quickly looked around the playground. No cats. No dogs. "Where did they go?" Nina asked.

"Listen," Cassidy said. "I hear something."

In the distance, the friends heard loud howling, followed by screeching. "Oh, my gosh," Nina said. "You don't think that huge dog is eating Gato for lunch do you?"

Jeff's face went pale. "I hope not, but we'd better find them right away."

The kids ran toward the sounds but stopped short when they came to the wooded area at the far end of the playground. Kids were never allowed to go in

there. "Mr. Morton told us to stay on the playground," Nina said.

Cassidy looked at her friend. "Do you want to find Gato?" she asked. "Or not?"

7
Into the Woods

Leaves tumbled in a whirlwind at their feet and a cold wind rattled the tops of the trees. "Rules are rules," Nina said.

"And they're meant to be broken in case of emergency," Cassidy told her.

"If we don't go in there, we may never find those people's pets," Jeff pointed out.

"And if we lose pets, we won't earn the money to help the poor animals at the shelter," Cassidy added.

"Worst of all," Jeff told Nina, "we won't find your grandmother's cat."

Nina nodded. "You're right," she said. "Let's go."

The three friends stepped into the dark shadows where the sun never reached. Tree limbs arched over them like long bony skeleton arms. A few reached out and snagged their clothes. Without the sun, it was cold. So cold that goose bumps scattered over their arms and up their backs. "Which way should we go?" Nina asked. She didn't know why, but she felt she had to whisper.

"Follow that trail," Jeff said, pointing to a faint dirt path that led between two trees.

"What I don't understand," Cassidy said as they made their way deeper into the woods, "is how Huxley and Cocomo got out of the classroom."

The kids had learned that the ghosts were stranded in the basement of Sleepy Hollow Elementary. They could only escape if something they owned back in their own time went with them.

"I think I know," Jeff said. He had read every ghost book in the library and considered himself an expert. "When the door opened, the Great Dane had Huxley's stick in his mouth."

"And the white cat had Cocomo's string," Nina said.

"That explains it," Cassidy said. "The only problem is, we have to find the stick and string or else the town of Sleepy Hollow will be haunted by two very active ghost animals."

Just then, a noise brought them to a halt. "Th . . . th . . . that didn't sound like a little kitty-cat," Nina whimpered.

"And it didn't sound like a dog, either," Jeff said.

The three friends stood as still as the trees in the forest. "It sounded," Cassidy said slowly, "like a human ghost!"

"Don't be silly," Nina said. "There aren't any ghosts in the woods. Are there?"

Jeff's face had gone a sickly shade of green. "Well, if a school basement can be haunted, why not a forest?"

"The school ghosts aren't dangerous," Nina pointed out. "So even if there ARE ghosts, we don't have to worry."

"Not all ghosts are friendly," Jeff said in a trembling voice.

"If Jeff is scared, then I'm scared," Cassidy said.

Back-to-back, the friends formed a tight circle so they could see in all directions.

Wooooooooooo.

The noise sounded like it was coming closer.

Woooooooooooo!

It was definitely getting louder.

WOOOOOOOOOOOOOOOOO!

"Run!" Cassidy screamed.

8
Lost

Cassidy ran right. Nina ran left. Jeff ran backward. After ten paces they all stopped, turned, and looked at each other.

"It's this way," Jeff said, pointing in one direction.

"No, it isn't," Nina said, pointing in another direction. "We have to go there."

"You're both wrong," Cassidy told them, pointing a third direction. "Let's go that way."

"We're lost in a forest, and we're about to be eaten by ghosts!" Nina screamed.

WOOOOOOOOOOOOOOOOOOOOOOOO!

Whatever was making the noise was nearly on top of them. Cassidy covered her eyes. Nina dropped to the ground and rolled into a ball. Jeff backed up

44

until he scratched against a dead tree's trunk.

A haunting voice seemed to come from every direction.

"Who dares to enter my forest?" moaned the voice.

Cassidy, Jeff, and Nina were too afraid to answer.

"Who is in our forest?" asked the voice again.

"This is the end," Nina said, covering her eyes. "I can't look!"

Cassidy tried to scream, but no sound came out. Jeff, on the other hand, pushed away from the tree and looked around. "Wait a minute," he said. "I know that voice."

Cassidy gulped a big breath. "You're right. It does sound familiar."

Nina peeked through her fingers. "It sounds like Ozzy," she said.

"Ozzy!" Jeff hollered. "Is that you?"

From high in the trees they heard the familiar laughter of their classroom ghost.

"Get down here right now," Cassidy said, getting mad.

In the small clearing beneath the trees, the air began to glitter like tiny dancing fireflies. The sparkles thickened until they finally took the shape of the ghost they knew all too well. Ozzy. But that wasn't all. Beside him another glitter cloud formed until the kids recognized Calliope. Tiny tears trickled down her

face to splash onto the ground. Ozzy wasn't crying. He was laughing.

"You should've seen the looks on your faces," Ozzy said between giggles.

"That wasn't funny," Nina said as she brushed leaves off the knees of her jeans. "Why are you here?"

Calliope's toes barely touched the ground as she floated toward the three friends. "Cocomo. Cocomo. I must find my Cocomo."

Ozzy blew past Calliope, causing the sad ghost to twirl through the air like a tumbleweed. When a tree got in her way, she went right through it.

"Calliope won't stop all that moaning unless we find her cat," Ozzy said. "I came to help her and to find Huxley."

"But . . . but . . . you can't leave the classroom," Cassidy said.

"Yes, they can," Jeff interrupted. "Cocomo and Huxley belong to them. As long as there's something that belongs to them out here, they can be here."

"You can't stay out for long," Cassidy warned the ghosts. The kids had learned the hard way that when ghosts wandered away from home they grew weaker and weaker until they almost disappeared.

"I won't go without Cocomo," cried Calliope. "We've been together forever! Don't make me go back without her."

Nina stepped toward the sad ghost. "I know exactly how you feel," she said. "My grandmother feels the same about Gato. Maybe if we work together, we can find all the missing pets faster."

"Good plan," Cassidy said. "Which way should we go?"

Before they could take a step, something came crashing through the forest. It sounded big and it was heading straight for them.

"That's not a ghost," Nina said. "It's a monster!"

9
Monster

"We're all going to get eaten by a monster!" Nina yelled and grabbed Jeff's arm. "This is why Mr. Morton told us to stay on the playground."

Jeff shook his head. "We have a secret weapon. Ozzy and Calliope will help us."

"Don't look at me," Ozzy said. "I'm out of here."

Calliope and Ozzy popped out of sight, leaving the three kids alone in the dark woods.

"So much for secret weapons," Cassidy said with a groan.

"Ahhh!" Nina screamed. "It's got me!"

"What?" Cassidy cried. "Is it a giant invisible monster?"

"Is it another ghost?" Jeff said, swatting the air around Nina.

"No," Nina said, slapping at her leg. "There was a huge spider crawling on my pants."

Cassidy groaned. "You scared me to death for a spider?"

Nina's face turned red. "It was a very big spider."

"We don't have time to worry about that now," Jeff told the girls. "The monster is just on the other side of those bushes."

Nina gulped as the bushes shook. In

terror, the friends stared as the bushes slowly parted. What kind of monster lived in these woods?

"You guys might want to wait around and get eaten, but I'm out of here," Cassidy said.

Nina nodded and pointed. "The school is this way. Let's go!" The three kids ran in the opposite direction from the monster. The faster they went, the faster the monster seemed to run. When they stopped to rest, so did the monster.

"I thought you said the school was this way," Jeff said, panting from all the running. Sweat popped out on his forehead and he wiped it away with his T-shirt.

"It was," Nina said slowly.

Cassidy groaned. "The school hasn't moved."

"No," Jeff said, grabbing a piece of broken tree limb off the ground to use as a weapon. "But the monster has." Crash! The monster broke through the trees and fell onto Nina. Her screams echoed throughout the woods.

10
Ouch!

Nina rolled on the ground. She kicked and she hit with all her might.

"Ouch!" screamed the monster.

OUCH? What kind of monster said ouch? Nina stopped fighting and looked at the monster. "Andrew!" she shouted. "You're no monster."

Cassidy disagreed. "Oh, yes he is."

Jeff pulled Nina up from the ground. "Andrew, what are you doing here?" Jeff asked.

Andrew knocked dried leaves off his shirt and frowned. "What are you doing in the woods? I heard Mr. Morton tell you not to leave the playground."

"But we heard the dogs and cats," Nina told him.

"Don't you mean dog and cat?" Andrew said.

"Sure," Jeff said, remembering that Andrew didn't know about the ghost dog and cat.

"You'd better get back to school before we tell on you," Cassidy said, trying to get rid of Andrew.

"If you don't let me look for the pets," Andrew said, hopping up from the dirt, "I'll tell Mr. Morton that you three disobeyed him."

Nina knew they had been caught. "Okay, let's just find those pets before anything else happens."

"Listen," Cassidy said. "I think I hear Huxley."

"Who's Huxley?" Andrew asked.

Jeff, Cassidy, and Nina ignored Andrew to listen. Sure enough, the ghost dog came sniffing around a tree. Only, Huxley's paws were nowhere near the ground. He floated even with Andrew's red ball cap, but Andrew had no idea the dog was there. Huxley's tongue hung out nearly to the ground, and Cassidy was certain he smiled at her.

"I don't hear a thing," Andrew huffed. "Now, which way did that big monster dog run?"

Nina had to stifle a giggle when Huxley sniffed Andrew's cap and it slipped down over Andrew's eyes. Her smile disappeared when the air sparkled nearby. Calliope and Ozzy popped into view.

Ozzy took one look at Huxley and

whooped. "My dog!" Ozzy said. "You found my dog."

"Admit it. You don't have a clue which way the animals went," Andrew said, unaware that Ozzy was hugging Huxley right above his head.

"We don't even know which way the school is," Cassidy said.

"If we don't find them soon, we're going to get trapped in the forest all night," Jeff said.

"We have to do something!" Nina said.

Ozzy was not a quiet kind of ghost, but he spoke in a soft voice. "Huxley can help," he said. Then he looked his dog right in the eyes. "Find Cocomo," Ozzy said. "Go get her."

Huxley gave a short yip and then flew through the forest.

"This way!" Jeff said.

The four kids pushed their way past the weeds and bushes to follow Huxley. He led them straight to the Great Dane, barking wildly at the foot of a very, very tall tree. Jeff grabbed the big dog's collar. "Boy, are we glad to see you," Jeff told the dog.

"But what about the cat?" Andrew said. "Did that dog eat it?"

Nina shook her head and pointed up,

up, up. Way in the very top of the big oak sat the white cat, meowing pitifully. Perched right beside her on the small branch sat Cocomo and Gato.

"Gato!" Nina called. "You come down here right now."

The orange cat didn't budge.

"What are we going to do?" Cassidy asked.

"We might
as well
go back
to school,"
Andrew said.

"There's no way we can get those two cats."

What Andrew didn't see was Cocomo, the third cat.

11
Ghost Deal

Calliope took one look at Cocomo and zoomed straight for the ghost cat. Calliope plucked her cat off the limb, and then, before heading back to the ground, pulled Cocomo's old piece of string from the white cat's mouth.

The white cat clawed at the string. Unfortunately, the movement made the branch crack. Gato and the white cat yowled as the branch gave way and they fell through the air.

"Gato!" screamed Nina.

Tail over head, Gato and the white cat dropped toward the ground.

"Watch out!" Cassidy yelled.

Andrew ducked, but Nina, Cassidy, and Jeff gathered together to form a

human net. The two cats landed right in their arms.

"Whew!" Cassidy said as she cuddled the white cat in her arms and tried to soothe her. "That was a close call."

"Too close for comfort," Nina said, holding Gato close to her and rubbing the orange cat's ears.

"At least every one is safe and sound," Jeff said.

"Except for one small problem," Nina said.

"What?" the kids all asked together.

"We're still lost!" she said. "Which way is the school?"

Cassidy looked left. Jeff looked right. Ozzy and Calliope shrugged.

Andrew looked behind him. "I'm sure it's this way. Follow me."

Andrew walked down the path. Jeff waited until he was out of hearing distance. Then he looked at his friends. "We're totally lost. But one of us can find the way out."

"Who?" Cassidy asked.

Jeff pointed to Ozzy's ghost dog. "Huxley is the best dog in the world," Jeff said. "And he's lived in that school for over one hundred years. If anybody can find the way back, it's him."

Jeff got down on his knees. He looked into Huxley's eyes. "Take us home, Huxley," Jeff said. "Take us home."

"*Woof*," Huxley answered. He started going in the opposite direction from Andrew.

"No, it's this way!" Nina yelled to their classmate. "And hurry!"

Andrew crashed down the trail after them as Huxley led them all to the safety of the school. They quickly bathed the

Great Dane and combed the burrs out of the white cat's tail before their owners showed up.

"Snickers looks like she had a wonderful time," the cat's man said. "She's so calm. As if she's been playing all day."

"Butterscotch looks like he's ready for bed," the Great Dane's lady said. "He's usually so full of energy I can't stop him. This is terrific!"

Cassidy, Nina, and Jeff smiled as the

man and woman each made a big donation to the animal shelter.

"This is a great idea," they both said. "I hope you do this again. We'll be sure to come back."

The kids cleaned up the classroom and put the mops in the hall closet. Nina cuddled Gato in her arms. The orange cat purred, happy to be safe again. "My *abuela* will be so glad to see Gato," she said.

Jeff sighed. "I think I know how she feels. I wish I had a pet of my own, but my mother said no with a capital *N*."

"You really want a dog, don't you?" Cassidy asked her friend.

"More than anything," Jeff said with a sigh.

Just then, the air behind them glittered. It swirled and twirled until Ozzy took shape. Next to him panted Huxley.

"Did you really mean it?" Ozzy asked Jeff.

"Mean what?" Jeff asked.

"When we were in the woods you said Huxley was the best dog in the world," Ozzy reminded him. "Did you mean it?"

"I meant it," Jeff said. "Huxley is one of the reasons I want a dog. He's loyal. He's fun. He's your best friend. I wish I had a dog just like him."

Ozzy looked down at his dog. Then he looked at Jeff. "If you really feel that way, then I'll share him with you."

"What?" Jeff asked.

The kids were used to seeing Ozzy play lots of pranks. They were used to Ozzy causing trouble. They were not used to him being nice.

"You helped me find my dog today," Ozzy said. "I thank you for that. Besides, we're friends and friends share — even if one of them is a human and one is a ghost!"

"Thanks, Ozzy," Jeff said. "That's the nicest thing I've ever heard."

Ozzy grinned and pulled out a roll of paper. With a flick of his wrist, he unrolled it. "So it's a deal, partner. Now, I've made a little list of some things good ol' Huxley needs. You should buy him toys. Lots of toys. He likes to chase things. . . ."

Ozzy's list went on and on. Nina giggled. Jeff sighed.

"I have a feeling," Cassidy said, "that this friendship doesn't stand a *ghost* of a chance!"

About the Authors

Marcia Thornton Jones and Debbie Dadey got into the *spirit* of writing when they worked together at the same school in Lexington, Kentucky. Since then, Debbie has *haunted* several states. She currently *haunts* Ft. Collins, CO, with her three children, three dogs, and husband. There, she writes other books for children, like the Swamp Monster in Third Grade series. Marcia remains in Lexington, KY, where she lives with her husband and two cats. She also works on many other books, such as *Champ,* coming out soon. Debbie and Marcia have fun with spooky stories. They have scared themselves silly with The Adventures of the Bailey School Kids and The Bailey City Monsters series.